CW00967577

The Lying Games

Art Vulcan

Published by Art Vulcan, 2024.

This is a work of fiction. Similarities to real people, places, or events are entirely coincidental.

THE LYING GAMES

First edition. October 21, 2024.

Copyright © 2024 Art Vulcan.

ISBN: 979-8227371591

Written by Art Vulcan.

Table of Contents

Table of Contents

Chapter 1:

Julia answered her phone with a brisk "hello," expecting another work call to interrupt her morning jog. The voice on the other end didn't match the tone of her day. It was Brooke, a name from the distant past, a name she hadn't heard in years.

Brooke spoke in a tremble, "Julia, it's Taylor. She's gone." Julia's breath caught, her feet stumbling over the pavement. Taylor, the heart of their high school group, the one who could make anyone laugh, the one who knew everyone's secrets and always knew what to say. Dead. It was a punch in the gut she hadn't seen coming.

The rest of the day passed in a blur of shock and disbelief. Julia couldn't focus on the merger documents in front of her. Her mind kept wandering back to their school days, to the time when they were inseparable, sharing every little detail of their lives. How could someone so vibrant and full of life be gone?

Finally, the day of the funeral arrived, and Julia found herself dressed in black, feeling like a fraud as she stepped into the quiet solemnity of the church. The pews were filled with faces she hadn't seen in years, some aged by time and others etched with grief. She spotted Brooke first, her once fiery red hair now a muted auburn, her artist's hands clutching a wad of tissues. Nate was next to her, his detective's eyes scanning the room as if searching for clues in the sea of mourners. Dylan sat a few rows back, his shoulders hunched, looking more like the awkward

1

teen she remembered than the confident mogul she'd read about in the papers. And Kelsey, poised and polished, with a forced smile that didn't quite reach her eyes as she whispered to her well-dressed husband and two kids.

Julia took a seat next to Brooke, who offered a sad smile of recognition. The scent of lilies and old wood filled the air as the service began. She watched the slideshow of Taylor's life, feeling the weight of the years that had slipped away. The laughter in the photos, the shared moments, it all seemed so distant now. Brooke leaned in and whispered, "It doesn't seem real, does it?" Julia nodded, her throat tight with unshed tears.

Nate's eyes met hers as he took his place at the podium to speak. His words about Taylor's spirit and her ability to bring people together were punctuated by the occasional sniffle from the audience. Julia's gaze drifted to Dylan, who had always been the brains of their group. His glasses were slightly askew, and his hand trembled as he wiped at his nose. She wondered what he'd been through since they'd last seen each other. The spotlight on his success had often obscured the shy boy who'd been there for them all.

Kelsey stepped up next, her voice steady, but her hands clutching the podium tightly. She talked about Taylor's wild streak, the parties that had defined their youth, and the quiet moments of friendship that no one else knew about. Julia felt a pang of regret. She'd judged Kelsey for settling down so quickly, but maybe there was more to her life than the perfectly manicured lawns and charity luncheons she posted about on social media.

After the service, they all gathered at a nearby park, the same one where they'd spent countless weekends in their youth. The awkwardness was palpable as they exchanged forced smiles and half-hearted condolences. The banter was stilted, the laughter hollow. They were five people who had once been a tight-knit group, now standing in a circle, unsure of how to bridge the chasms that time and life had carved between them.

Julia found herself drawn to Dylan, who had retreated to the fringes of the gathering. She approached him with a tentative smile. "How are you holding up?" she asked, her voice gentle. He looked up, his eyes red-rimmed. "I don't know, Julia. It's all just... surreal." His gaze drifted over to the playground, where a group of children played, "Do you remember when we'd come here and dare each other to do the highest swing?"

Julia nodded, a small smile playing on her lips. "And you'd always go the highest, even though you were terrified of heights." Dylan's eyes focused on her, a glimmer of the old mischief shining through his grief. "You always knew how to push us." Julia felt a pang of nostalgia. "And Taylor knew how to catch us when we fell." Dylan's smile grew sad. "Yeah, she did." They watched the children's games in silence, the echoes of their own youth playing out before them.

Brooke joined them, her eyes red-rimmed but her expression thoughtful. "Do you guys ever wonder what happened to us?" she asked. Julia looked at her, surprised by the question. "What do you mean?" Brooke took a deep breath, "We were inseparable. And now... look at us." She gestured to the group, now huddled together, "We're just... strangers with a shared history."

Nate spoke up, his voice low. "You know, when I heard about Taylor, the first thing I thought was that it couldn't be true. That there had to be a mistake. She was the one who could handle anything." His words hung in the air, a subtle reminder of the unspoken tension that had always existed between him and Taylor. Julia knew that Taylor had had a crush on him back in the day, but Nate had never reciprocated. It was a wound that had never quite healed.

Kelsey's perfect facade cracked for a moment as she spoke next. "Remember that time we all snuck out to the lake and had that epic food fight?" Laughter rippled through the group, a welcome reprieve from the heaviness that had settled on them. Julia felt a twinge of nostalgia, recalling the sticky mess of ketchup and mayo on her favorite white shirt, the one she'd had to bury at the bottom of her drawer.

But as the chuckles faded, the silence grew heavy again. Brooke's eyes searched each of their faces. "Do you guys feel it too?" Julia's gaze snapped to hers, curiosity piqued. "Feel what?" Brooke took a shaky breath. "That something's not right." Nate's eyes narrowed, his detective instincts kicking in. "What are you talking about?"

Brooke leaned in closer, her voice a whisper. "The way Taylor died... it's not like her. She was always so full of life, so... fearless." Julia's stomach twisted. Fearless, yes, but not reckless. Taylor had a way of making everything seem like an adventure, but she wasn't the type to take stupid risks. "What do you mean?" she asked, her voice low.

Brooke took a deep breath. "Her apartment was spotless, like she knew she was leaving. It was like she just... stopped living." Nate's eyes narrowed. "What are you suggesting?" Brooke looked at her feet, then back up at them. "I don't know. But I have this feeling, deep in my gut, that we're missing something."

Julia felt the tension coil around the group like a tightening spring. "Maybe we should look into it," she said slowly. Nate frowned. "What do you mean?" Dylan spoke up, his voice tight. "Maybe there's more to her death than meets the eye." Kelsey's perfect smile slipped. "I can't believe it either. But if there's a chance..."

The conversation grew hushed as the realization of what they were suggesting sank in. Julia looked around at her friends, at the people she'd once known so well. They were all holding onto something, some piece of themselves that had been lost to time and distance. "Okay," she said firmly. "Let's do it. For Taylor."

They decided to gather for drinks the following evening, something that would be familiar yet allow them to talk openly. The bar they chose was a local spot they'd frequented back in high school, a place where the neon lights cast a nostalgic glow over the worn booths. As they settled in, the old dynamics began to reassert themselves. Brooke was still the passionate one, her eyes lighting up as she spoke about her art, but with a newfound sadness in her voice. Nate, the skeptic, was now the voice of caution, his detective instincts telling him there was more to the story. Dylan remained the intellectual, his words measured and thoughtful, but now with a hint of vulnerability that Julia hadn't seen before. And Kelsey, ever the organizer, had already pulled out her phone to create a group chat for them to share information.

Chapter 2:

The conversation flowed easily at first, reminiscing about the pranks they'd pulled, the all-nighters studying for finals, and the heartaches they'd endured. But as they recounted their memories, Julia noticed something peculiar. There were moments in their shared past that no one seemed to remember in the same way. Small details that didn't quite align. Taylor's smile in the photos seemed to hold secrets she'd never shared. Julia's thoughts drifted to the call she'd received about Taylor's death. The way the news had hit her, like a surprise sucker punch, didn't feel right. It was as if something was nudging at her, telling her that there was more to the story.

"Do you guys remember the night of senior prom?" Julia asked, swirling the ice in her whiskey. Nods around the table, smiles tinged with nostalgia. "Taylor looked stunning, didn't she?" Dylan nodded. "I never told her, but she was the belle of the ball that night."

Kelsey spoke up, "And the after-party at her place?" The group chuckled, recalling the night filled with music, confetti, and teenage angst. But as the smiles grew dimmer, Julia couldn't shake the feeling that there was something more to uncover. She took a sip of her drink, the whiskey burning down her throat. "But do you guys remember what happened after the party?"

Brooke leaned in, her eyes searching. "What do you mean?" Julia's gaze flicked to Nate, who was watching her intently.

"Taylor had that weird look on her face, right before we left. Like she knew something we didn't." The room grew still, the buzz of the bar fading into the background. Nate spoke slowly, his detective instincts honed. "You think she was hiding something?" Julia nodded. "It's just a feeling. But the way she looked at us that night... it was like she was saying goodbye without actually saying it."

Dylan's eyes searched hers, the ghost of a question lingering. "What could she have been hiding?" Kelsey's voice was soft, but the concern was clear. Julia took a deep breath. "I don't know. But we were all there. Maybe we can piece it together." They fell into a tense silence, the air thick with the weight of their suspicion.

The evening progressed, the whispers of their past mingling with the clinking of glasses and the hum of the bar. Julia couldn't shake the feeling that they were all holding onto something, a shared secret that had been buried with Taylor. As they talked, the holes in their memories grew more apparent, like Swiss cheese with every piece of cheese representing a lost piece of their youth.

"You know, I can't remember much about that night after prom," Kelsey admitted, her eyes distant. "Everything's such a blur." Nate leaned forward, his gaze intense. "But something happened, didn't it?" His words hung in the air like an unanswered question, a silent accusation. The group exchanged nervous glances. Julia felt the walls closing in around her, the whispers of doubt echoing in her mind.

Dylan spoke up, his voice unsteady. "I remember finding her in the kitchen, talking to someone on the phone." Julia nodded, the memory coming back to her in fragments. "It was late. She looked upset." Nate's eyes narrowed. "And what about after that?"

Brooke's voice was barely audible. "I think we all left separately. I can't recall anyone else being there." The room felt smaller, the air thick with tension.

Julia's thoughts raced. What had happened that night? Why couldn't she remember? "Taylor's death," she began, her voice barely a whisper, "do you guys think it was an accident?" The question hung in the air like a storm cloud.

Nate leaned back, his eyes searching hers. "The cops couldn't find a clear cause," he said, his voice measured. "They're calling it 'suspicious circumstances'. But without more evidence..." He trailed off, leaving the words unspoken. The implication was clear: Taylor's death was a puzzle with missing pieces.

Dylan's hand tightened around his glass. "What are we saying here?" His voice cracked. "That someone... hurt Taylor?" The room grew colder as the unthinkable took root in their minds.

Brooke's eyes filled with tears. "Why would anyone do that?" Julia's thoughts raced. "We need to figure this out." she said, her voice firm.

The following night, the four of them gathered again, this time in the privacy of Nate's apartment. They sat in a circle, the room lit by the flicker of candles, shadows dancing on the walls. Nate pulled out a notepad and pen, his detective's instincts in full gear. "Okay," he began, "Let's go through everything we remember about that night."

Julia took a deep breath, her heart racing. "Let's start with the party." Kelsey nodded, her eyes glazed with memory. "It was perfect. Just like Taylor to throw something so... magical." Dylan leaned forward, his elbows on his knees. "But you know what? I don't think any of us were really okay that night."

Nate's gaze swept over each of them, his expression unreadable. "Okay, let's break it down. What do you remember happening after the party?" Julia felt the weight of his scrutiny, her thoughts racing to that night. "Well, she was on the phone. I just thought it was a fight with her boyfriend at the time." Dylan's eyes met hers, his gaze piercing. "But what if it wasn't?"

Kelsey spoke up, her voice shaky. "I remember leaving early because I had a curfew." She paused, her eyes filling with tears. "I never knew what happened after that. I've always wondered..." The room was quiet, each person lost in their own thoughts. Julia's mind was racing. "What if that night at the party... something went wrong?" she murmured.

Nate cleared his throat. "What do you mean, Julia?" His voice was gruff, but his eyes held a hint of concern. "Well, we all had our fair share of secrets," she began, looking around at her friends. "What if there was something that none of us knew about?" The room grew tense, the air thick with the scent of unspoken words.

"You think someone hurt her?" Dylan's voice was low, his eyes wide with shock. "It's possible," Julia replied, her own voice trembling. "But why now? Why after all these years?" Brooke wiped a tear from her cheek. "Maybe it was always meant to happen. Maybe we just didn't see it coming."

Nate shifted in his chair, his discomfort palpable. "Look, I know we've all got our suspicions, but let's not jump to conclusions. The cops found no signs of foul play." Julia leaned in, her eyes searching Nate's. "But you said it yourself, the cause of death was suspicious. What aren't you telling us?"

He sighed, rubbing his temples. "There were some things that didn't add up. The coroner couldn't pinpoint it, but..."

something felt off." The room was silent, each person wrestling with their own fears. "What do you think it could be?" Kelsey's voice was barely above a whisper. Julia felt a chill run down her spine.

Brooke spoke up, her voice trembling. "Remember the night we found those old letters in Taylor's room?" Nate's head snapped up, his eyes sharp. "What letters?" Julia's heart raced as the forgotten memory surfaced. "The ones from her mom," Brooke said, her voice a mix of pain and accusation. "The ones she said she burned but never did."

Chapter 3:

"The letters," Julia murmured, the words bringing a rush of images to her mind—Taylor's mother's handwriting, the secrets spilled onto the pages. "What if... what if it's related?" Kelsey's hand flew to her mouth, her eyes wide with horror. "Her mom's been dead for years." Dylan's eyes searched the room. "But what if someone else found them? Someone who didn't want those secrets out?"

Nate leaned forward, his face etched with concern. "Guys, we're getting ahead of ourselves." But his protest was met with silence, the gravity of the situation settling over them like a shroud. "Look," Julia said, her voice steady, "We need to know everything. If we're going to get to the bottom of this, we can't hold anything back."

Dylan nodded, his eyes never leaving Julia's. "Okay. That night, after prom, I saw something." He took a deep breath, his hands trembling slightly. "I saw Taylor with... with someone." His voice trailed off, and Julia's stomach dropped. "Who?" she asked, her heart racing. Dylan swallowed hard. "I don't know. It was too dark, but it definitely wasn't anyone from school."

Brooke's eyes widened. "What are you saying?" Kelsey leaned in, her grip on her glass tightening. "Did you tell the cops?" Nate's question was sharp, his pen hovering over the notepad. "No," Dylan replied, his gaze darting around the room. "I didn't want to get anyone in trouble. And I didn't know if it was important."

Julia's mind raced, the puzzle pieces slowly coming together. "But what if it was?" she asked, her voice low. "What if whatever was in those letters was connected to her death?" Kelsey's hand trembled as she set down her drink. "We need to find them." Nate's expression grew grave. "We can't just go digging through a dead girl's things. That's not how this works." Julia's gaze didn't waver. "But what if it's the key to understanding what happened?"

"Understanding won't bring her back," he said, his voice tight. "But it might give us some closure," Brooke said softly. Nate sighed, the weight of their words pressing down on him. "Okay. But we need to be careful. If there's something there, it's probably not going to be pretty."

They decided to start with Taylor's apartment. Julia felt a knot in her stomach as they approached the familiar building, the night air cold against her skin. The place looked the same as it had in her memories, but there was a stillness that felt eerie. They let themselves in with a spare key Brooke had kept, the door creaking open to reveal the spotless living room. "It's like she knew," Kelsey murmured. "Like she was expecting us."

Julia walked down the hall, her eyes lingering on the closed door to Taylor's bedroom. She could feel the others watching her, their footsteps muffled by the carpet. "You guys go ahead," she said, her voice tight. "I need a minute." They nodded, their expressions a mix of understanding and concern.

Once alone, Julia pulled out her phone, scrolling through the messages she'd ignored for weeks. Taylor's name was like a neon sign, a constant reminder of her own neglect. The first message was a simple "Hey, we need to talk." Then, a week later, "It's important, Julia." And finally, two days before the fateful call, "It's about the letters." Julia's stomach lurched. Letters? What could she have meant?

Julia walked into the bedroom, her eyes scanning the room. Everything was neat and organized, just like Taylor. The smell of her favorite perfume still lingered, a ghostly presence that brought a fresh wave of pain. She spotted a shoebox on the top shelf of the closet, pushed back into the corner. Her heart racing, she climbed on a chair to retrieve it.

"What did you find?" Kelsey called from the living room. Julia's hands trembled as she opened the box, revealing a stack of yellowed letters. "Guys, she was trying to reach me before..." she trailed off, her voice cracking. The letters were addressed to Taylor from her mother, the return address from a town none of them had ever heard of. Nate joined her, peering over her shoulder. "What are these?" Julia handed him the phone, the messages displayed for all to see. "Taylor had been trying to tell me something. I ignored her." The room grew silent as the weight of her confession sank in. Dylan's eyes searched hers. "What could it have been?"

"Let's start with these," Brooke said, holding up the letters. They gathered around the bed, each taking one. Julia felt the paper, brittle with age, and began to read. The words were a jumble of accusations and confessions, a tapestry of pain and regret. "Her mother was hiding something," she murmured. "And Taylor knew." Nate's eyes scanned the pages, his brow furrowed. "These are intense. What could it be?" He handed a letter to Julia. "This one's about a man named James." Julia's heart skipped a beat. "James?" The name was vaguely familiar, but she couldn't place it.

Julia began to read, her eyes widening with each line. The letter spoke of a love affair, a secret child, and a promise never to reveal the truth. "This can't be," she murmured. "Taylor had a brother?" The room grew still as they digested the revelation.

"But why would that lead to her death?" Kelsey's voice was tremulous. Julia's eyes scanned the letter, her thoughts racing. "Maybe she found out something about James," she murmured. "Something that put her in danger." Brooke took a deep breath. "We need to find out who James is." Nate nodded. "And why it was such a secret." Julia felt the guilt coil tighter in her stomach. "Taylor was reaching out to me," she admitted, her voice barely a whisper. "Just before she... she sent me messages, saying it was important. But I was busy with work, and I kept putting it off."

The group decided to stay in town for a few days, driven by an unspoken need to uncover the truth. Nate offered to use his detective connections to gain access to Taylor's case file. "I can't ignore this," he said, his voice firm. "If there's anything that can give us closure, we have to find it." Julia nodded, the guilt of ignoring Taylor's messages still fresh in her mind.

Chapter 4:

The following morning, Nate called Julia with an update. "I've got the file," he said, his voice tight with anticipation. "Meet me at the park. We'll go through it together." Julia felt a rush of nerves as she agreed. The park where they'd shared so many memories with Taylor now held the promise of uncovering the mystery surrounding her death.

As they spread the case documents on a picnic table, the sun peeked through the trees, casting dappled light across the pages. "It looks like she'd been interviewing people from high school," Nate said, flipping through the reports. Julia's eyes widened. "What could she have been looking for?"

"It's like she was piecing together a puzzle," Brooke murmured, her eyes scanning a page. "But why would she do that?" Dylan's voice was thick with confusion. "Maybe she found something that scared her," Kelsey suggested, her grip tightening on the letters. They fell into a tense silence, each lost in their own thoughts.

Julia's eyes scanned the documents, her legal mind racing. "Look at this," she said, pointing to a highlighted section. "Taylor had been reaching out to people from our high school, asking about the night of the prom." Nate leaned in, his eyes narrowing. "What's she looking for?" Julia's voice was tight. "I don't know, but it's like she was trying to warn us."

Dylan pulled out his laptop, his fingers flying over the keys. "Let me see if I can access her emails," he said, his expression intense. Within minutes, he had hacked into Taylor's account. "Look," he said, turning the screen towards them. "These messages are to someone called 'The Ghost'. They're encrypted."

Julia leaned in, her curiosity piqued. "What could they be about?" Nate's brow furrowed as he skimmed through the emails. "It's like she was onto something big," he murmured. "But why keep it from us?" Brooke's eyes searched the screen, her voice barely above a whisper. "Maybe she didn't trust us."

"Or maybe she was protecting us," Julia suggested, her eyes scanning the encrypted messages. "Look at the dates." She pointed at the screen. "Taylor reached out to each of us before she... before it happened." The realization hit them like a sledgehammer. Taylor had tried to warn them, but they'd all been too caught up in their own lives to listen.

Nate's jaw clenched. "We need to find out who this 'Ghost' is." He picked up his phone, dialing a number. "I've got a friend in forensics. Maybe he can crack this encryption." While they waited for his call to connect, the group sat in silence, the only sound the distant laughter of children playing.

The line clicked over, and Nate spoke quickly, explaining the situation in hushed tones. Julia watched him, her heart racing. Dylan's eyes were glued to the screen, scrolling through more emails, his mind racing. Brooke leaned against the table, her gaze unfocused. "What if... what if this James is the 'Ghost'?" Kelsey's voice was shaky. "What if he's been watching us?"

The call ended abruptly, Nate's expression grim. "We've got to keep this quiet," he said, his voice low. "We don't know who we can trust." Julia nodded, her heart pounding. They had to be careful; Taylor had clearly been onto something dangerous.

"Let's split up," Nate suggested, his eyes darting around the park. "Dylan, keep working on the emails. Julia, you and I will go through the case file." Brooke nodded, her eyes dark with determination. "Kelsey and I will start reaching out to people from school, see if anyone knows anything."

Kelsey's hand trembled as she pulled out her phone. "I'll start with the ones I still talk to." Julia's gaze was glued to the encrypted screen, the name "The Ghost" taunting her. What had Taylor found that had been worth dying for? As the group dispersed, the gravity of their mission settled heavily on their shoulders.

"You okay?" Dylan whispered to Kelsey as they walked away from the table. She nodded, her eyes misty. "Just... thinking about Taylor." But the truth was, the whispers of their past were growing louder, echoing through her mind. She hadn't told anyone about her struggles with substance abuse back then, not even Julia. Taylor had been her rock, her secret keeper.

Chapter 5:

Julia couldn't shake the feeling that there was something Kelsey wasn't telling them. As they drove to their old high school, she finally broke the silence. "You know, after the prom night, Taylor was there for me when things got bad," Kelsey said, her voice wavering. "I had a... a problem." Julia's eyes remained on the road, her grip tight on the steering wheel. "What kind of problem?"

Kelsey took a deep breath, her eyes meeting Julia's briefly before looking away. "Substance abuse," she whispered. "I never talked about it, not even with you guys." Julia felt a twinge of guilt. How could she have missed it? "Taylor helped me through it. She was the one who got me into rehab when no one else knew." Dylan's eyes widened in the rearview mirror. "Why didn't you tell us?" Kelsey's smile was sad. "I was ashamed. But she never judged me. She just... she was always there."

Julia's thoughts spun. "If Taylor was helping you, that means she had a reason to be secretive, right?" Kelsey nodded. "Yeah, she was worried about me. But it was more than that." They pulled into the school's parking lot, the sight of the old building bringing a rush of memories. "What do you mean?" Julia asked, her voice gentle.

"Remember how she was always so protective of me?" Kelsey's eyes searched Julia's. "It was like she had a sixth sense for when I was in trouble." They stepped out of the car, the crunch

18

of gravel underfoot echoing the weight of their words. "But it wasn't just me," Kelsey continued, her voice shaking. "Taylor knew all of our secrets. And she kept them."

Julia nodded, her eyes misting over. "Yeah, she was always the one who held us together." They walked towards the school, the hollowness of the building mirroring the emptiness in their hearts. "But why would someone want to hurt her for that?" Dylan's question hung in the air, unanswered.

Brooke's voice was quiet when she finally spoke up. "Guys, I need to tell you something too." She took a deep breath, her eyes on the ground. "Taylor and I had a fight before graduation." Julia stopped, her eyes widening. "What?" Brooke looked up, her gaze meeting each of theirs in turn. "It was about Mr. Daniels."

"The math teacher?" Nate's eyebrows shot up. "What about him?" Julia felt the blood drain from her face as she remembered the rumors that had swirled around Mr. Daniels back in high school. Brooke nodded, her voice barely above a whisper. "Taylor caught me with him. She was so mad. She said I was going to ruin my life, that it was wrong." Julia's mind raced, trying to piece together the timeline. "When was this?"

"Right before graduation," Brooke said, her eyes welling up. "I was devastated. I didn't know what to do. But she made me promise to end it." Dylan's hand rested on her shoulder. "Did you?" Brooke nodded, her eyes downcast. "Yeah, I did. But it was hard. I was so in love with him. And then, when he was fired..." Julia's stomach twisted. "Fired? What happened?"

Brooke took a deep, shaky breath. "He was fired because of Taylor. She had evidence, something she'd found. She showed it to the school board." Nate's eyes widened. "And he just disappeared?"

"Yeah," Brooke said, her voice barely a whisper. "He left town. I never saw him again. And I hated Taylor for it." Nate's eyes searched hers, his grip tightening on the case file. "But she did it to protect you," he said gently. "You know that."

"I know," Brooke murmured, her eyes filling with tears. "But I couldn't forgive her. And now she's... gone." Julia wrapped an arm around her, the weight of their shared grief heavy between them. "We're going to find out what happened, Brooke. I promise." They continued their walk down the hallways of the empty school, each step echoing off the lockers. The smell of dust and old memories filled the air.

Julia's thoughts turned to the encrypted emails and the mysterious 'Ghost'. Could it be someone from their past, someone they'd trusted? The guilt over ignoring Taylor's calls gnawed at her. "What if we missed something?" she murmured. Nate glanced at her, his eyes serious. "We can't change that now, Julia. But we can find out the truth."

As they sat in the empty classroom, the silence was pierced by the distant sound of a locker slamming shut. Julia jumped, her nerves on edge. "You think it's someone following us?" she whispered. Nate shrugged. "Could be. We should be careful." They divided the case file between them, each page revealing more about Taylor's investigation.

Julia's eyes fell on an interview with a former teacher, Mrs. Jenkins. "Taylor talked to her," she murmured. "Remember how she was always in her office?" Nate nodded. "Yeah, she had a soft spot for Taylor." Kelsey's voice was shaky. "But why would she be relevant?" Julia's mind raced, piecing together the scattered threads of their memories.

"Guys," she said slowly, "what if... what if Taylor was looking into something bigger than just our personal lives?" They exchanged glances, the gravity of her words sinking in. "What do you mean?" Dylan's voice was skeptical. "What could be bigger than our secrets?" Julia took a deep breath. "What if she found something that threatened all of us?" Nate's eyes searched hers, understanding dawning. "The Ghost," he murmured. "It's gotta be someone who's connected to all of us. Someone who knew about the letters and had something to hide." Julia nodded, her mind racing. "But who? And why would they hurt Taylor?"

"I don't know," Kelsey said, her voice shaking. "But we have to find out." They spent the rest of the afternoon at the school, talking to teachers who had known Taylor and digging through old yearbooks. The name "The Ghost" remained elusive, but the feeling of being watched grew stronger.

Chapter 6:

Julia couldn't shake the thought that one of them was hiding something. The name "The Ghost" echoed in her mind, a specter from their past that now seemed eerily connected to Taylor's tragic end. She watched her friends closely, their faces a tableau of grief and determination. Was one of them hiding behind that moniker?

"Guys," she said, her voice cutting through the silence of the classroom. "We can't ignore the possibility that The Ghost is someone we know." Brooke's eyes snapped to hers, a flicker of fear crossing her features. "What are you saying, Julia?"

"Look at it this way," Julia continued, her eyes scanning the documents before her. "Taylor was investigating something. Something she thought was important enough to reach out to all of us about. And she was killed." Dylan's eyes narrowed as he processed her words. "You think someone we all know is involved?"

"I don't know," Julia admitted, her voice tight with tension. "But we can't ignore the possibility. The Ghost... it's got to be someone who knew about the letters, someone with a motive." She glanced around the room, her gaze lingering on each of her friends. "Someone who knew her secrets, and maybe even ours."

Nate flipped through the pages of the case file, his eyes narrowing. "But who? And why would they do this?" Dylan's gaze was focused on his laptop, his fingers tapping away. "I've decoded the first email," he said, turning the screen towards them. "It's about a meeting. Taylor had set up a meeting with The Ghost."

"A meeting?" Kelsey's eyes widened. "What could they have talked about?" Julia leaned in, reading over Dylan's shoulder. "It doesn't say," he murmured. "But it's definitely about the letters." The name "The Ghost" seemed to hover in the air between them, a specter of suspicion. "We need to find out who this person is," Brooke said, her voice firm. "And fast." Nate nodded, his expression grim. "Agreed. We can't just sit around waiting for answers to fall into our laps." They decided to retrace Taylor's steps, starting with her last known whereabouts before her death.

The café where Taylor had arranged to meet The Ghost was a quaint place on the outskirts of town. As they sat in a booth, Julia felt a shiver run down her spine. "It's like she's still here," she whispered. Kelsey nodded, her eyes misty. "Remember how she used to love coming here to study?" They ordered coffee, the bitter scent wafting through the air, a poignant reminder of their lost friend.

"Okay," Nate said, his voice firm. "We need to think like Taylor. Who would she have talked to before coming here?" Dylan tapped on his laptop. "I've been checking her phone logs," he said, his eyes scanning the screen. "Her last call was to a number registered to a payphone."

"A payphone?" Kelsey frowned. "That's so... old school." Brooke's eyes lit up. "But it's also untraceable. She must have had a reason to be so secretive." Julia's mind raced. "The Ghost could have used a burner phone, something that couldn't be traced back to them."

Nate nodded. "It's a good point. We need to find that payphone." They split up, each taking a different direction to canvass the area for any clues. Julia's thoughts swirled as she walked, her eyes scanning every alley and corner. Who could be behind this? Was it someone they had once trusted?

"Hey, Julia!" Dylan called, waving her over to a narrow side street. "I think I've found it." The group gathered around the old, graffitied phone booth, a relic of a bygone era. The glass was shattered, the receiver dangling by a thread. Julia felt a shiver run down her spine, the reality of Taylor's final moments becoming eerily tangible.

"This is where she made the call," Dylan said, his voice tight with emotion. "But why a payphone?" Brooke mused. "It's like something out of a spy movie." Nate nodded. "Exactly. The Ghost knew what they were doing, leaving no digital footprint." Julia's eyes searched the surrounding area, her mind racing. "Taylor had to have been scared," she murmured. "But she was so brave."

"We need to find out who she was supposed to meet here," Kelsey said, her voice barely above a whisper. "Someone who knew enough to use a payphone." Julia nodded, her eyes on the shattered booth. "The Ghost," she murmured.

"But why the secrecy?" Dylan's question hung in the air, thick with tension. "What were they talking about that was so dangerous?" Nate's eyes searched the area, as if expecting to find a clue in the discarded coffee cups and cigarette butts littering the ground. "Whatever it was, it got her killed."

Julia stepped into the phone booth, her hand shaking as she picked up the receiver. "It's dead," she murmured, replacing it with a clunk. The echo of the dial tone in the silence was chilling. "We need to find out who this 'Ghost' is," she said, her voice firm. "And what they wanted with Taylor." Brooke leaned against the booth, her eyes scanning the street. "But where do we even begin?" she asked, her voice filled with frustration. "This town isn't that big," Nate said, his eyes narrowed. "Someone must have seen something." Julia nodded, her mind racing. "We need to talk to everyone we can, retrace her steps."

They decided to split up again, each taking a section of town to question. Nate's phone buzzed with a message from his contact at the precinct. "The Ghost," he murmured, reading the text. "It's a pseudonym used by someone who's been blackmailing students for years." Julia's heart sank. "What does that mean?" she asked. Nate's eyes were grim. "It means Taylor wasn't just looking into our secrets. She was poking a hornet's nest."

"Blackmail?" Brooke's voice was incredulous. "Who would do something like that?" Kelsey's eyes were wide with shock. "But why? Why would someone target our school?" Nate's gaze was intense as he read through the message again. "It says the blackmail started around the time we were juniors. They had something on everyone—grades, personal relationships, you name it."

Chapter 7:

Julia felt a cold dread spread through her. "So, Taylor was trying to expose The Ghost?" Nate nodded. "It looks like it. And she was getting close." He handed her the phone. The text message was short but packed with explosive information. Julia's mind raced, recalling the whispers that had haunted their high school hallways. "Cheating scandals, drug busts, college admissions," she murmured, the memories flooding back. "They were all connected to anonymous tips. Everyone thought it was just rumors."

Brooke's eyes widened. "But if Taylor had real evidence..." Her voice trailed off, the implications too horrifying to voice. "We need to find out who else The Ghost had on their hook," Dylan said, his voice tight. "We can't let them get away with this."

Julia nodded, her mind racing. "We need to think back to senior year," she said. "Who were the people most affected by those scandals?" They gathered around Nate, huddling over the phone as he called in more favors, asking for any information on the anonymous tips that had rocked their school. "Cheating scandals, drug deals..." he murmured, listing off the events that had changed their lives.

"Remember Becky?" Brooke's voice was low. "Her scholarship was revoked because of those rumors." Julia's eyes widened. "You think she could have something to do with this?" Dylan leaned in, his eyes on the screen. "Look at the dates," he said, pointing to a string of emails. "The blackmail coincides with Becky's downfall."

Nate nodded, his expression grim. "But it doesn't stop there," he said, scrolling through the messages. "There's a pattern. The Ghost targeted students who had something to lose." Julia felt the blood drain from her face as she realized the implications. "So, Taylor was getting too close?" Dylan's voice was tense. "Looks like it," Nate said, his eyes on the screen. "This person had a lot of power over everyone."

Brooke leaned in, her eyes wide. "But why would they want to meet Taylor here?" she asked, her voice trembling. "What did she know?" Kelsey's eyes searched the street, as if expecting The Ghost to appear at any moment. "Maybe she had something on them," she said, her voice barely above a whisper. "Something that could have brought them down."

Julia nodded, her mind racing. "We need to retrace her steps," she said firmly. "Find out who she talked to, what she found out." Nate's phone buzzed again, and he read the message with a furrowed brow. "They're sending over a list of all the people The Ghost blackmailed," he said. "It's... it's a long list."

The names scrolled down the screen, each one a potential suspect. Julia's heart raced as she scanned through them, her eyes catching on familiar names from their high school days. "Becky's on here," she murmured. "And... Mr. Daniels?" Nate nodded, his jaw tight. "The list goes on," he said, scrolling through the endless names. "They had dirt on everyone."

"But why?" Kelsey's voice was small. "Why go through all that trouble?" Julia's eyes searched the screen, her mind racing. "Power," she murmured. "Or money." The group exchanged looks, the reality of their situation sinking in. The Ghost had been manipulating their lives for years, and Taylor had been the one to finally try to stop them. "It's... it's sickening," Brooke said, her voice shaking. "How could someone do this?" Dylan's eyes were hard as he studied the list. "Because they could," he said, his voice cold. "They had everyone's secrets. Everyone was afraid."

"But we can't let them win," Julia said, her voice firm. "Taylor was trying to do the right thing. We owe it to her to finish what she started." Nate nodded, his jaw clenched. "We're going to find out who The Ghost is," he said. "And we're going to bring them down." They divided the list, each taking a few names to investigate. The weight of their task was heavy, but their determination was stronger.

"I'll talk to Becky," Brooke volunteered, her eyes on the name. "We were close before everything fell apart." Julia's gaze was thoughtful. "I'll look into Mr. Daniels," she said, her voice tight. "See if he's back in town." Dylan took a deep breath. "I'll check out the others."

Julia and Nate headed to the local library, the only place they could think of to start their search. The smell of old books and the quiet hum of the air conditioner seemed to amplify their whispers. "How could we not have known?" Nate's voice was low. Julia's eyes were on the floor, lost in thought. "We were all just trying to survive high school," she said, her voice barely above a murmur. "We had our own stuff to deal with."

"But Taylor," Nate said, his voice thick with emotion. "She saw it all. And she was trying to fix it." Julia nodded, her eyes misty. "Yeah," she whispered. "And now she's gone." They sat down at a table, the list of names before them. "We all have to admit it," Julia said, her voice shaking. "At some point, we all benefited from The Ghost's silence."

"But that doesn't mean we can't do the right thing now," Nate said, his gaze intense. "Taylor was trying to protect us, even when we didn't know we needed it." Kelsey's voice was soft. "But what if The Ghost had something on her, too?" The room went quiet, the question hanging in the air like a dark cloud.

Julia pushed the thought aside. "We'll deal with that if it comes up," she said, her voice firm. "For now, let's focus on finding out who they are." They spent hours in the library, piecing together a timeline of events from that fateful senior year. Each name on the list brought back a flood of memories—some painful, some embarrassing, and others just sad.

As the sun set outside, they decided to take a break and reconvene at Julia's apartment. The drive was tense, the silence between them a stark reminder of their mission. They gathered in the living room, each with new information. "Becky's been clean for five years," Brooke said, her voice tight. "But she's still haunted by what happened." Julia nodded, her eyes on the floor. "Mr. Daniels is back in town," she murmured. "He's been working at a community college, keeping a low profile."

Nate leaned forward, his eyes on the notes spread out before them. "And the others?" They took turns sharing what they had found: a series of tragic stories, each one a piece of a puzzle that painted a grim picture of The Ghost's reach. "They all had something to hide," Julia said, her voice heavy. "But none of them seem capable of murder."

The silence that followed was thick with doubt and fear. "Maybe we're looking at this the wrong way," Dylan suggested. "What if it's not just one person?" Julia's heart skipped a beat. "A network?" The possibility was terrifying, but it made sense. The

Ghost had been too good at keeping their identity hidden, too skilled at playing their twisted game.

"A network," Nate echoed, tapping his pen against the table. "It would explain the power, the reach." Kelsey's eyes widened. "But who would be involved in something like that?" Julia's mind raced. "Someone who had something to gain," she murmured. "Or someone who was forced."

Chapter 8:

They decided to pool their information and look for connections between the blackmail victims. As they laid out their findings, a pattern began to emerge—each person on the list had something in common with the others, a thread that wove through their high school lives like an invisible web. "They were all popular," Julia said, her voice tinged with disbelief. "Or at least, well-connected."

Dylan nodded, his eyes scanning the notes. "And each one of them had something to protect—their reputation, their future." Nate leaned back in his chair, his brow furrowed. "So, The Ghost wasn't just targeting individuals, but the fabric of our school's social hierarchy." Kelsey's hand trembled as she spoke. "It's like we were all puppets, and The Ghost was the master puppeteer."

The room was quiet as they digested the gravity of their discovery. Julia stood, pacing the floor, her mind racing. "We need to find the thread that connects all of these people," she said, her voice determined. "The common link." Nate nodded, his eyes never leaving hers. "We're getting closer," he assured her.

The group huddled around the coffee table, their notes spread out like a map of their past. Julia's hand hovered over a name, her heart racing. "Mr. Daniels," she murmured. "He had a motive. And he's been living under a new identity for years." Nate nodded gravely. "But we can't jump to conclusions," he warned. "We need hard evidence."

Brooke leaned in, her eyes scanning the timeline. "What if Taylor found something that could have exposed the entire network?" she suggested. The room fell silent, the implications sinking in. Dylan spoke up, his voice tense. "We need to go back to the prom night," he said, his eyes on the floor. "There's something we're missing."

Julia nodded, her mind racing. "We'll retrace our steps," she said, her voice firm. "Talk to everyone who was there, see if anyone noticed anything out of the ordinary." They divided the list of prom attendees among themselves, each taking on a few names to contact. The weight of their task felt heavier with every passing minute.

As they worked, Julia couldn't help but feel the tension growing between them. Nate shot Dylan a sideways glance, his expression unreadable. Dylan, for his part, seemed lost in thought, his fingers tapping a nervous rhythm on the arm of the chair. Julia knew Nate was suspicious of Dylan's technical expertise, his ability to navigate the digital world in a way that could have allowed him to be The Ghost. And she couldn't ignore the nagging doubt in her own mind about Brooke's relationship with Mr. Daniels.

"Brooke," Julia said, her voice tentative. "Can we talk about prom night again?" Brooke's eyes met hers, a flicker of something unreadable passing through them. "What about it?" she asked, her tone guarded. Julia took a deep breath. "Your relationship with Mr. Daniels... Just how close were you two?"

The room grew colder, the air thick with unspoken accusations. Brooke's cheeks flushed, and she looked away. "It's not what you think," she murmured. "But you were the one who said we need to be honest with each other," Julia pressed, her eyes searching Brooke's. "Was there something you weren't telling us?"

Brooke took a deep breath, her eyes filling with tears. "It was just... flirty," she said, her voice shaking. "He was older, and I was just a kid. I didn't know what I was doing." Julia's stomach twisted, her thoughts racing. "But you talked about the prom night argument," she said, her voice gentle. "That's not just flirty."

Brooke nodded, her gaze on the floor. "I know," she murmured. "But I never meant for it to go this far. I never knew he could be involved in something like this." Julia reached out, placing a hand on Brooke's arm. "It's okay," she said. "We just need to get to the bottom of this." Kelsey's eyes flicked between them, her suspicion of Brooke clear.

Meanwhile, Dylan's fingers flew over his keyboard, searching for any digital breadcrumbs that could lead them to The Ghost. Nate watched him, his thoughts racing. Could Dylan have been the mastermind behind it all? His expertise was undeniable, and he had the means to keep their secrets buried. Julia noticed the tension and cleared her throat. "Guys, we need to stay focused."

Nate nodded, pushing his suspicions aside for now. "Julia's right," he said, his eyes on Dylan. "Let's stick to the plan." Dylan looked up, his expression unreadable. "I'm with you," he said, his eyes meeting Nate's. "We're all in this together." The room felt charged, the air thick with unspoken accusations and fear.

Julia's gaze was focused on her notebook, her pen moving rapidly as she made notes. "Brooke," she said, her voice gentle but firm. "Can you think of anyone else who might have had a vendetta against Taylor?" Brooke's eyes searched hers, and Julia could see the turmoil within. "There was... someone," she said finally. "But I don't know if it's relevant."

The room went quiet, the tension palpable. "Who?" Nate's question was almost a demand. Brooke took a deep breath. "His name was Marcus," she said, her voice low. "He was in love with Taylor, and she... she didn't feel the same way." Julia's heart sank. "What happened?"

Brooke's eyes searched the floor. "They had a bad breakup right before prom. He was devastated, started acting out, and eventually dropped out of school." Julia felt the pieces of the puzzle shifting, creating a more complex picture. "Could he have become The Ghost?" she asked, her voice tentative. Nate's gaze was on Dylan, who had gone still, his fingers hovering over the keyboard. "It's possible," he said slowly. "But we still need proof."

Chapter 9:

The next few days were a whirlwind of interviews and dead ends. Each person they talked to had a different memory of prom night, each one more fragmented than the last. It was as if the very fabric of their past was unraveling before their eyes. And Kelsey—Kelsey's behavior grew more erratic with each passing day. Her eyes darted around the room, her hands never still, her speech rapid-fire. Julia couldn't shake the feeling that something was off.

One evening, as they debriefed at Julia's apartment, Kelsey burst in, her breathing ragged. "Guys," she said, her voice shaking. "I found something." She slapped a crumpled piece of paper on the table, her eyes wild. It was a note, scrawled in Taylor's handwriting. "It's a list of names," she said, her voice trembling. "And it's got a date and a location. I think it's where she was going to meet The Ghost."

Julia's heart raced as she smoothed out the paper, her eyes scanning the list. Each name brought a new wave of dread—friends, enemies, teachers. The Ghost had indeed targeted everyone. But the last name on the list sent a cold shiver down her spine: Marcus. "Could he be involved?" she murmured. Nate's gaze was sharp. "It's definitely worth looking into," he said, his eyes on Kelsey.

Brooke's eyes searched Kelsey's, her concern growing. "You okay?" she asked softly. Kelsey's nod was too quick, her smile forced. "Yeah," she said, her voice too bright. "Just... just tired." But the tremor in her hands and the sheen of sweat on her forehead told a different story. Julia felt a knot in her stomach. What if Kelsey had something to do with this? Her history with substance abuse made her vulnerable, a potential pawn in The Ghost's twisted game.

Nate cleared his throat, breaking the silence. "We need to talk to Marcus," he said, his eyes on the note. "But carefully." Julia nodded, her mind racing. "And we need to keep an eye on Kelsey," she said, her voice low. "Her behavior... it's not right."

The group exchanged glances, the unspoken question hanging in the air. Could Kelsey have had a hand in Taylor's death? The thought was too much to bear. They had been friends for so long, had been through so much together. But the evidence was mounting, and the doubt was growing. Julia decided to confront Kelsey directly. "Hey, Kels," she said, her voice gentle. "We need to talk." Kelsey's eyes darted around the room, her smile slipping for just a moment before she reined it back in. "What about?" she asked, her voice high-pitched. Julia took a deep breath. "Your behavior," Julia said. "It's just... it's not like you."

Brooke stepped closer, her eyes filled with concern. "We just want to make sure you're okay," she said, her voice gentle. But Kelsey's eyes flashed with something that looked suspiciously like anger. "I'm fine," she snapped. "Just... stressed." Julia's stomach knotted. Kelsey had always been the wild one, but this was different. This was desperation. "What aren't you telling us?" she asked, her voice soft but firm. Kelsey's hands shook as she reached for her phone, her eyes never leaving Julia's. "Nothing," she said, her voice brittle. "Just... just let me handle my part of the investigation."

The room was silent, the air charged with mistrust. Dylan spoke up, his voice measured. "Guys, we can't let our suspicions get the better of us." But Julia couldn't shake the feeling that there was something Kelsey wasn't saying, something that could blow their whole investigation apart.

Brooke's eyes searched Kelsey's, looking for any sign of the friend they had known for so long. "We just want to help," she said, her voice laced with tension. Kelsey's smile was brittle. "I know," she replied, her hands shaking. "But I can handle this." She grabbed the note and headed for the door. "I'll track down Marcus," she said over her shoulder. "You guys keep digging."

The moment the door closed, the room erupted in whispers. "What's going on with her?" Brooke asked, her eyes wide. "It's like she's on something," Dylan murmured. Nate's gaze was hard. "Her addiction," he said, his voice low. "It's possible she's using again."

Julia felt a wave of dread wash over her. "We can't let this ruin us," she said, her voice firm. "We need to stick together and find out who The Ghost is." The others nodded, their expressions grim. They had come so far, uncovered so much, but now the trust between them was frayed. Each of them had secrets they hadn't shared, secrets that could now threaten to tear them apart.

They decided to split up for the night, each of them needing space to process the revelations of the day. Julia watched as her friends left, one by one. She couldn't shake the feeling that they were being watched, that The Ghost knew they were closing in.

As she lay in bed that night, Julia's mind raced with scenarios. Could Kelsey have relapsed? Was she hiding something? And what about the others? Every shared secret felt like a potential motive. The walls of her apartment seemed to close in, suffocating her with doubt and fear. She knew she needed to keep her suspicions in check, but the nagging feeling that one of them was responsible for Taylor's death grew stronger with each passing moment.

Chapter 10:

T he next day, the group met again, the tension palpable. They were no longer the carefree friends they had once been; they had become detectives in a twisted game where everyone was a suspect. They decided to proceed with caution, each one of them aware of the potential danger lurking beneath the surface. Julia's eyes searched her friends' faces, looking for any sign of deceit or fear.

As they divvied up tasks, Kelsey remained unusually silent, her eyes darting around the room as if searching for an escape. The others exchanged concerned glances, their whispers about her behavior growing louder. "We need to keep her close," Brooke murmured. "If she's in trouble, we can help." Julia nodded, her mind racing. But she couldn't shake the thought that Kelsey could be the one they were searching for.

Dylan decided to check the prom night footage, hoping it would provide some clue to The Ghost's identity. "It's got to be in the archives," he said, his voice tinged with hope. "We might finally get some answers." Nate agreed, his eyes never leaving Kelsey. "But let's not jump to conclusions," he cautioned. "We all have secrets."

Julia couldn't shake the feeling that something was off with Kelsey, so she along with the others decided to follow her after the meeting. She watched as Kelsey wandered the streets, her movements erratic, her eyes darting around nervously. Julia's heart raced as she trailed her friend, the weight of her suspicion like a lead balloon in her chest.

They arrived at the gym in their old high school, the once-proud gymnasium now a shell of its former glory. The paint was peeling, the equipment windows were broken. The sight of it brought back a flood of memories, the ghosts of their past coming alive in the shadows. "What are we doing here?" Nate asked, his voice low as they approached the front steps.

Julia swallowed hard. "This is where it all started to unravel," she murmured. "The after-prom party." The others nodded, their expressions a mix of dread and determination. They had all been there that night, the night when Taylor had first started to suspect something was wrong. The night when their friendship had begun to fracture.

The gym door creaked open, the sound echoing through the empty hallways. The once-shiny hardwood floor was now scuffed and dull, the air thick with dust and forgotten dreams. Julia stepped inside, her heart pounding in her chest. The others followed, their footsteps echoing in the cavernous space.

Memories flooded back—the laughter, the tears, the screams. The smell of sweat and spilled drinks still lingered in the air, a ghostly reminder of the night that had changed everything. They moved through the gym in silence, their eyes scanning the space for any clue, any hint of what had happened here that could lead them to The Ghost.

The bleachers creaked as they climbed them, their feet echoing on the metal. Julia's stomach turned as she remembered the feeling of sitting here with Taylor, their heads leaning on each other's shoulders, whispering about their futures. It was here that their friendship had begun to crack, a fissure that had grown into a chasm over the years.

They reached the spot where the makeshift stage had been set up, the place where the band had played until the early hours of the morning. Julia could almost hear the throb of the bass, the shrill laughter of her friends as they danced the night away. But amidst the shadows, there was something else, something darker.

"We can't remember that night," Brooke murmured, her voice barely audible. "But I know something happened here." Julia nodded, her eyes scanning the space. The pact they had made to keep their secret buried was as much a part of the gym as the peeling paint and the dust.

Nate leaned against the stage, his eyes distant. "The Lying Game," he said, his voice low. "We were so stupid." Julia felt a chill run down her spine as she recalled the drunken whispers and the vow of silence. Each of them had revealed something damaging, something that could ruin lives. But the night had ended with more than just secrets—it had ended with a bond that had held them together through the years, despite the fractures in their relationships.

As they stood there, the gym's ghosts whispered their forgotten confessions. Julia's mind was a whirlwind of images—Kelsey's tears, Brooke's anger, Dylan's confession about his father's gambling debts. And Taylor, her laughter silenced by fear. The game had been a twisted attempt at trust, a way to ensure they had dirt on each other, a bond that no one could ever break. But the fear in Taylor's eyes that night had been real, and it was a fear that had never truly left them.

The floorboards groaned underfoot as they moved closer to the spot where the drinks had been spilled and the truths had been told. Julia felt the weight of those secrets pressing down on her, a heavy burden that had shaped their lives more than they cared to admit. She could almost hear the echoes of their slurred voices, the desperation in their confessions. It was a night they had all tried to bury, but now it was clawing its way back to the surface.

Brooke's hand tightened around Julia's arm as she whispered, "Do you remember what you said that night?" Julia's eyes searched hers, the question unspoken. They had all shared something damning that night, something that could ruin their futures if it ever got out. The room seemed to pulse with the beat of a distant heart, the secrets trapped within its walls, demanding to be heard.

Dylan leaned in, his voice a harsh whisper. "The things we said... they were just drunken ramblings," he insisted, his eyes darting around the room. But Julia knew better. The Lying Game had been more than just a game—it was a pact sealed in fear and regret. They had all sworn to keep each other's secrets, to protect one another from the consequences of their confessions. But now, with Taylor's death, that pact was unraveling.

Julia's mind reeled with the fragments of memory that had resurfaced since their investigation had begun. The prom night was a jigsaw puzzle with missing pieces, each friend's recollections slightly different, as if the whispers of the gym had altered their truths over time. The neon lights, the throb of the bass, the scent of spilled drinks—these sensory echoes remained, yet the crucial moments remained elusive.

Chapter 11:

A s they stood in the dimly lit gym, the air thick with the dust of forgotten memories, they each tried to piece together their own version of events. The whispers of their past seemed to swirl around them, a cacophony of voices that grew louder, more insistent, with each step they took closer to the spot where the game had played out. Julia's heart raced, her breath shallow. What had she said that night? What had she promised to protect?

Brooke's eyes searched the floor as if the answers were hidden in the dusty cracks between the floorboards. "It's like we all remember different versions of the same night," she murmured. "But we can't all be right." Nate nodded, his brow furrowed. "Maybe we don't remember because we don't want to," he said, his voice low. "Maybe it's easier to forget than to face what we did."

Julia felt a knot tighten in her stomach. What had she been so desperate to hide? What had Taylor discovered that had led to her death? They had to find the truth, no matter how much it hurt.

They searched the gym, their eyes peeled for any clue that could lead them to Taylor's secret. It was Dylan who noticed it first—a loose floorboard, slightly out of place. Nate pried it up with a crowbar from his car, revealing a hidden compartment beneath. The air grew colder as they stared into the dark space.

"Guys," he murmured, his voice shaking slightly. "I think we've found something."

Julia's heart raced as she shone her phone's flashlight into the void. The beam illuminated a stack of envelopes, a USB drive, and a tattered journal—Taylor's handwriting scrawled across each page. The room felt as if it were closing in, the whispers of their past echoing louder. "This is it," Julia said, her voice shaking. "This is what she was hiding."

The documents were a timeline of 'The Ghost's' reign of terror, each entry a dark chapter in the school's history. The group exchanged horrified glances as they realized the extent of the blackmail—how it had shaped their lives, twisted the school's social hierarchy, and left a trail of broken souls in its wake. Taylor had been meticulous in her research, connecting the dots that led to Mr. Daniels, Becky, and several others. But there was one name that stood out, one that none of them had ever expected to see.

"Kelsey?" Julia whispered, her voice shaking as she read aloud from a page. The room went still, the air thick with accusation. The journal entry detailed a secret meeting, a desperate exchange of information for silence. Kelsey's name was written in Taylor's shaky hand, along with the words "The Ghost's pawn?" The color drained from Brooke's face as she reached for the journal, her eyes scanning the pages. "No," she breathed. "It can't be."

But as they dug deeper into the evidence, the pieces began to fit together. The encrypted emails, the burner phone calls, the sudden changes in Kelsey's behavior—it all pointed to one conclusion. Their friend had been manipulated, her vulnerabilities exploited by the very enemy they had sworn to unmask. "We have to talk to her," Julia said, her voice firm. "We can't let her go down for this."

The group approached Kelsey's house with a mix of trepidation and determination. The lights were off, the curtains drawn. Julia's hand hovered over the doorbell, her heart pounding in her chest. The moment she pressed it, the house erupted into chaos.

Kelsey's frantic voice echoed through the hallways. "What the heck do you want?" she screamed, her words slurred. They could hear the sound of glass shattering. They burst through the door to find Kelsey huddled in a corner, surrounded by shards of a broken vase, her eyes wide and crazed. The room was in disarray, with papers strewn everywhere and a faint smell of alcohol in the air.

Julia's eyes searched the room, her heart racing. "What's going on?" she asked, her voice trembling. Kelsey's eyes darted around, finally landing on the pile of documents and photos on the floor. "You," she spat, her voice filled with accusation. "You're going to ruin everything."

The group exchanged confused glances as they approached the scattered evidence. Each page was a puzzle piece in Taylor's quest to uncover the truth. Julia picked up a photo of Mr. Daniels, his face contorted in rage. "What is this?" she asked, her voice shaking.

Kelsey stumbled to her feet, her eyes wild. "You don't understand," she slurred. "It's all connected." Her hand reached for a crumpled envelope, her trembling fingers smoothing out the wrinkles. The note inside was a confession from Becky, admitting to her role in the scholarship scandal. "The Ghost," Kelsey whispered. "He had it all."

Julia's heart raced as she pieced the puzzle together. Taylor had been gathering evidence, building a case against the blackmailer who had haunted their school. But it was all just out of reach, the details hazy, memories obscured by the fog of time and fear. "Kelsey, tell us what you know," Julia urged, her voice gentle but firm.

The room was a whirlwind of accusations and confusion. Kelsey's eyes darted from one friend to another, her hand shaking as she clutched the incriminating evidence. "I don't know," she whispered. "But he has eyes everywhere."

Chapter 12:

Suddenly, the room plunged into darkness. The sound of a phone vibrating pierced the silence, sending a bolt of fear through the air. Julia fumbled for her device, the screen illuminating an anonymous text: "Leave it alone, or you'll end up like Taylor." The message was short, but the threat was clear. They had gotten too close.

Kelsey's breath hitched in her throat, her grip on the envelopes tightening. The room felt colder, the air thick with unspoken accusations and the heavy weight of the truth they were unraveling. "We can't," Julia murmured, her eyes on the phone. "We have to find out who did this."

The sound of the text echoed in the stillness, each syllable a warning. They were being watched, and The Ghost knew they were getting closer. Nate's voice was firm. "The police and I will take care of this," he said, his hand on Julia's shoulder. " You guys need to stop, This isn't a game anymore."

Julia's eyes searched his, her mind racing. "We can't just stop," she said, her voice shaking. "Taylor didn't." But the fear in her eyes was unmistakable. They were in over their heads, and now they had a direct threat. Dylan's voice was quiet, his words cutting through the tension. "We have to get out of here," he said, his eyes darting to the window. "We're not safe."

Nate stepped forward, his hand on Dylan's arm. "No," he said firmly. "We go to the police." But Dylan's gaze was fixed on the phone, his expression unyielding. "They won't help us," he murmured. "They're in on it." The room grew colder, the air thick with accusations and fear. Brooke's hand clutched at her chest, her breath coming in shallow gasps. "What do we do?" she whispered.

Julia stepped into the fray, her eyes flashing with determination. "We can't leave," she said, her voice firm. "We have to see this through." But Nate's grip on her arm was tight, his eyes filled with a fear she hadn't seen since prom night. "Julia," he said, his voice low. "This isn't just about us anymore. The Ghost will stop at nothing to protect his secrets."

Kelsey's hand trembled as she held up the envelopes, the evidence of their shared past. "We can't just walk away," she murmured. "We owe it to Taylor." Her eyes searched Julia's, and for a moment, Julia saw the ghost of the girl she had once known—vulnerable, lost, desperate for the truth. "But we can't do it alone," Kelsey added, her voice shaking. "We're all in this together."

The room grew quiet as the implication of Kelsey's words sank in. They had all played the Lying Game, had all held each other's fates in their hands. And now, those secrets were being used against them. Julia felt a cold sweat break out on her forehead as she read the first text. It was from the night of the prom, a confession she had hoped was lost to time. But here it was, in stark, digital letters, a reminder of the pact they had made.

Brooke's hand flew to her mouth as she read her own text. The words seemed to burn into her skin. "It's starting," she whispered, her eyes wide with terror. "The Ghost is playing with us."

Kelsey nodded, her face ashen. "We can't stop now," she said, her voice barely audible. "We're so close." The room was silent except for the distant wail of a siren, a mournful echo of the chaos they had unleashed.

Julia's phone buzzed again, the screen lighting up with a chilling message. "I know about the baby," it read, and the blood drained from her face. The room spun around her as the secrets they had buried surfaced like a rotting corpse in a lake. Each text was a dagger to the heart, a reminder of the lies they had told to protect themselves.

"What does it mean?" Brooke's voice was a tremor in the silence. Julia could see the fear in her eyes, the reflection of her own panic. The words on her screen seemed to pulse with malevolent intent. "It's from The Ghost," she murmured. "And it's about my abortion back in highschool" The room grew colder, the whispers of the past swirling around them like a tornado of accusation.

The texts kept coming, each one more personal, more damning than the last. They had all lied, all played the game, and now the truth was being used as a weapon. Dylan's phone buzzed, and he read it aloud, his voice cracking. "I know about the money and the theft." The room grew colder as the gravity of the situation settled over them.

"We need to figure out who's sending these," Julia said, her eyes darting around the room. "They have to be close to us, someone who knows our past." The air was thick with accusation and fear. The whispers of their forgotten confessions seemed to echo through the gym, turning the space into a prison of their own making.

The texts continued to bombard their phones, each message more personal, more threatening. "It's like we're in a game of Clue," Dylan said, his voice shaky. "But instead of Colonel Mustard with a candlestick in the library, it's our lives on the line." They had all played the Lying Game, but now, the game was playing them. The Ghost was a master manipulator, turning their secrets into deadly ammo.

Julia felt the walls closing in, the weight of their shared past suffocating her. "We have to figure out who knew about our secrets," she said, her voice strained. "Someone was there that night." They had all been too busy running from their own demons to realize the monster they had created together.

They gathered in Julia's living room, the tension thick enough to cut with a knife. Each of them had a theory, a suspect, but no one was willing to voice their suspicions. The texts had stopped, but the silence was deafening. It was as if the ghosts of their past had been given a megaphone, and every secret they had whispered in the dark was now being shouted in their faces.

Julia's mind raced as she tried to piece together the puzzle. Taylor had been the first to die, and now they were all being hunted. She knew they were getting closer to the truth, but she also knew that the closer they got, the more dangerous the game would become. They had to find a way to expose The Ghost before it was too late.

Her eyes fell on the journal once more, her heart racing as she read through the pages. The entries grew more frantic as the date of their high school reunion approached, detailing Taylor's fears and suspicions. Julia's breath hitched as she reached the final entry. "They can't find out," it read. "I'll tell everyone at the reunion."

Chapter 13:

T he pieces of the puzzle clicked into place. Taylor had been gathering evidence to expose The Ghost, to free them all from the prison of their shared guilt and secrets. But she had been silenced before she could. Julia's eyes snapped up, meeting the others'. "The reunion," she said, her voice cold. "That's when Taylor was going to tell everyone."

The room was a tapestry of shocked expressions and furtive glances. They had all been so focused on their own fears and suspicions that they had missed the most crucial piece of the puzzle. It was right there, in the pages of Taylor's journal—her final, desperate attempt to set things right. "Someone didn't want that to happen," Brooke murmured, her eyes dark with understanding.

Julia nodded, her thoughts racing. "The letters," she whispered, her eyes never leaving the page. "Taylor mentioned them before she...before." The letters from James, the secret half-brother none of them knew about. Could it be that he was the one they had been searching for all along? The Ghost, their tormentor, their judge and jury, lurking in the shadows of their past.

The room grew colder, the whispers of the texts on their phones fading into the background. Julia felt a chill run down her spine as she turned the page, her eyes scanning the words that seemed to jump out at her. The handwriting grew more frantic, the ink smudging with the desperation of each confession. And then she saw it—a revelation that made her blood run cold. "Julia," Taylor had written. "James isn't just my half-brother. He's yours too."

The room spun as Julia's hand trembled, the journal slipping from her grasp and hitting the floor with a thud. The others leaned in, their eyes wide with shock as they read over her shoulder. "What the hell?" Nate murmured, his hand reaching out to steady her.

Julia's mind raced as the implications of the journal entry sank in. Her father, the man she had trusted, the one who had always been there for her—how could he be involved in this? The whispers of the gym, the shadows of their past, had been leading them down a twisted path, and now, the most unthinkable of truths lay before them.

Her eyes searched her friends' faces, but the words wouldn't come. How could she tell them that the man they had all known as Mr. Castellanos was the one they had been looking for? The one who had manipulated their lives, who had held their secrets in his grip like a puppet master pulling strings? The silence was deafening, the air in the room heavy with the weight of her revelation.

"What are you talking about?" Brooke finally spoke up, her voice trembling. Julia took a deep breath, her mind racing as she tried to form coherent thoughts. "Taylor found out about James," she began, her voice shaking. "But she didn't just find out that he was her half-brother. She found out that he was mine, too." The room felt like it was spinning, the walls closing in on them as the truth began to take shape.

Kelsey's hand flew to her mouth, her eyes wide with shock. "Mr. Castellanos?" she murmured, her voice barely above a whisper. "Your dad?" Julia nodded, unable to find the words to explain the betrayal she felt. The man who had walked her to her prom, who had held her when she cried over college rejections, was the very monster they had been searching for. It was a revelation that shook the foundations of her world, leaving her feeling unsteady and unsure of who she could trust.

Brooke's eyes searched Julia's, the color draining from her cheeks. "But why?" she asked, her voice shaking. "Why would he do this?" The question hung in the air, heavy and unanswered. Julia's mind was a tornado of thoughts, whirling with the chaos of memories and suspicions. Her father had always had a strange obsession with the school's drama, but she had never imagined it could be this twisted.

The group sat in stunned silence, each one trying to piece together the implications of Julia's revelation. It was Dylan who spoke first, his voice shaky. "We need to get this to the police," he said, his eyes on the journal. "We have to expose him."

Julia's hand hovered over the page, her mind racing. "But what if it's not just him?" she whispered. "What if there's more to this?" The others exchanged glances, the gravity of the situation settling over them like a dark cloud. The Ghost had woven a web so intricate, so pervasive, that they had all been ensnared in it without even realizing.

They had been playing the Lying Game for so long, hiding their secrets from each other, that it had become second nature. But now, the game had turned deadly, and the stakes were higher than ever.

Julia's eyes searched her friends' faces, each of them a reflection of the betrayal she felt. She knew that confronting her father would be the hardest thing she'd ever done, but she couldn't ignore the evidence in front of her. The whispers of their past had led them to this moment, and the truth was staring her in the face. "We need to talk to him," she said, her voice barely above a whisper.

Chapter 14:

They approached Mr. Castellanos's house with a mix of anger and fear. The man who had been their mentor, their confidant, was now a monster in their eyes. The porch light flickered as they stepped onto the creaking boards, the shadows playing tricks on their minds. Julia's hand was shaking as she rang the doorbell, the echo of their friendship's end resonating in the quiet night.

Her father answered the door, his face a mask of surprise and confusion. "Julia?" he said, his eyes darting to the group behind her. "What's going on?" His voice was a shaky facade of innocence.

Julia took a deep breath, her heart racing. "We know about James," she said, her voice steady despite the turmoil in her chest. "We know about the blackmail, the lies, the game." She watched as his expression morphed from shock to guilt, then to anger.

Her father's eyes narrowed, his hand tightening around the doorframe. "What are you talking about?" he growled, his voice a thunderclap in the quiet night. But Julia could see the fear in his eyes, the way he glanced over her shoulder at her friends, the journal clutched in her hand.

"The letters," she said, her voice unwavering. "The ones Taylor found. The ones about James." The name hung in the air, a specter from the past come to claim its due. Mr. Castellanos's face paled, the facade of innocence crumbling like dust. "You had a son," Julia accused, her voice shaking with rage and betrayal. "And you kept it hidden from everyone."

Her father's eyes darted from Julia to her friends, their accusatory gazes like knives cutting through the deception. "It was a mistake," he said, his voice strained. "A mistake I've been trying to fix for years." His words hung in the air, a confession wrapped in the guise of a justification. But Julia saw the cracks in his armor, the desperation in his eyes.

"What kind of mistake?" Brooke demanded, her voice shaking with anger. "What could be so bad that you would go to these lengths? You killed Taylor in cold blood!" The air grew colder as Mr. Castellanos took a step back, the doorway framing his silhouette in the dimly lit hallway.

Her father's eyes grew wide, the veins in his neck pulsing with the strain of keeping his secrets buried. "It was an accident," he choked out. "I never meant for anyone to get hurt. It was just..." His words trailed off, his eyes pleading with Julia to understand, to forgive. But she could only see the man who had used his power and influence to manipulate their lives, to keep his dirty secrets hidden.

"Tell us everything," Julia demanded, her voice a whip-crack of accusation. "Or we go to the police."

Her father's gaze fell to the journal in her hand, and he swallowed hard. "Years ago," he began, his voice low and pained. "Before James was born, I had an affair with a woman in town. She was pregnant, and I didn't want anyone to know. I was afraid of losing everything—my family, my job, my reputation." His eyes searched hers, desperate for a shred of understanding.

Julia felt a cold rage building inside her. "So you just abandoned them?" she spat. "Left them to deal with the mess you made?"

Mr. Castellanos nodded, his eyes filled with regret. "When James came looking for me, I was terrified. I couldn't let anyone know the truth, not even your mother." His voice cracked. "I thought I had it all under control, but then Taylor started poking around. She was so close, Julia. She had found out about James, about the blackmail." His eyes grew distant, lost in the memories of his dark deeds.

Julia felt a chill run down her spine as she pieced the puzzle together. Her father had killed her half-brother, had buried his guilt in the shadows of their lives, and had used their shared history to control them all. "Why?" she whispered, the question echoing in the tense silence. "Why would you do this?"

Mr. Castellanos looked at her with a mix of regret and resignation. "I didn't mean to," he said, his voice strained. "It was an accident. James had found out, and he was going to expose me. He came to the school, and we argued. It was a fight that got out of hand. I didn't mean for him to die." His eyes searched hers, begging for understanding.

Julia's heart felt like it was shattering into a million pieces. "Why?" she whispered. "Why didn't you just come clean?" The silence grew heavier, the weight of his secrets pressing down on them like a leaden shroud. "I was scared," he murmured. "I didn't know what to do. I thought if I could just keep it all hidden..."

The words hung in the air, unspoken but understood. Julia's father had been living a double life, using his power and influence to bury his indiscretions. He had killed James, not out of malice, but out of fear and desperation. And when Taylor had stumbled upon the truth, he had seen no other way out than to silence her permanently. "What about Taylor?" Julia's voice was barely a whisper, her hand clutching the journal to her chest like a shield against the horror of the revelation.

Chapter 15:

Mr. Castellanos looked away, unable to meet her eyes. "When Taylor found those letters, she started poking around. She was getting too close. I had to protect my family, my legacy. I didn't mean for it to go that far." His voice was a broken whisper, the truth choking him. "I hired someone to scare her, to make her stop. But it...it got out of hand. They killed her instead." The confession hung in the air, a heavy shroud of guilt and despair.

Julia felt the color drain from her face as she stared at her father, the man she had looked up to her whole life, now revealed to be a killer. "How could you?" she choked out, her voice trembling with emotion.

Her father's eyes were filled with a deep sadness that seemed to swallow the light around them. "I'm sorry," he whispered. "I never wanted any of this to happen." His shoulders slumped, and for a moment, Julia saw a glimpse of the man she had once known—kind, caring, a pillar of the community. But that man was gone, replaced by a monster who had destroyed lives to protect his own.

"You have to turn yourself in," Julia said, her voice firm despite the tremble in her chest. "This ends now." Mr. Castellanos looked at her, his eyes brimming with tears. "I can't," he said, his voice cracking. "I can't face what I've done."

Julia felt a wave of anger crash over her, mixing with the sadness that threatened to drown her. "You have to," she insisted. "For Taylor, for James, for all of us. You can't keep living this lie."

Her father took a step back, his hand reaching for the door to close it. "I'm sorry, Julia," he murmured. "I never wanted you to find out like this." The door clicked shut, leaving Julia and her friends on the porch, staring at the cold, unyielding wood.

Brooke's hand found Julia's, her grip tight and reassuring. "We have to go to the police," she said firmly. "We can't let him get away with this."

Julia nodded, feeling the weight of her father's confession like a boulder on her chest. "We can't let him," she agreed. The group turned away from the house, the shadows playing tricks with their emotions. They had come seeking answers, but the revelation had left them feeling more lost than ever.

As they walked back to their cars, the whispers of their past seemed to follow them, echoing through the quiet streets like a mournful chant. Each step was heavier than the last, their friendship forever changed by the dark secrets that had been unearthed. They had all played the Lying Game, but none of them had known the true cost of winning.

Brooke's eyes were red from crying, and Dylan looked ready to collapse under the weight of the truth. "I can't believe it," she murmured. "Mr. Castellanos, of all people." The words were a knot in her throat, a betrayal she couldn't fully comprehend. They had all been so naive, thinking that their high school drama was nothing more than a distant memory.

Kelsey was silent, her thoughts racing as she tried to make sense of the web of deceit that had been spun around them. Her own secrets felt trivial now, in the face of what they had uncovered. She had never imagined that the Lying Game they had played all those years ago could lead to something so dark, so twisted.

The group piled into Julia's car, the journal and its damning contents hidden safely away. As Julia pulled out of the driveway, the headlights cutting through the night, she felt the gravity of what they were about to do. They were going to shatter the illusion they had all lived under for so long. The silence in the car was deafening, each of them lost in their own tumult of emotions.

When they arrived at the station, the fluorescent lights felt harsh and unforgiving. They filed into a small, cold room, the kind reserved for those who bore witness to the darker side of life. Julia placed the journal on the table, the pages whispering of their secrets. The detective assigned to Taylor's case, a stoic woman named Detective Ramirez, raised an eyebrow as she opened it, her eyes scanning the pages with a mix of skepticism and curiosity.

One by one, they recounted their findings, their voices shaking with the weight of their words. Julia spoke of her father's confession, her voice thick with betrayal and pain. Dylan shared their suspicions about James and the blackmail, his voice tight with anger. Brooke spoke of the threats they had received, her voice a tremble of fear. And Kelsey, her eyes never leaving the detective's face, revealed her own part in the Lying Game, her secrets spilling out like a dam finally breaking.

Detective Ramirez listened with a stoic expression, her eyes flickering between the journal and the group. Julia could see the wheels turning in her mind, piecing together the puzzle they had laid before her. "You're telling me that Mr. Castellanos, a well-respected member of this community, has been blackmailing you all?" she asked, her voice measured. "And that he killed Taylor and James to keep his secrets hidden?"

Julia nodded, her throat tight with emotion. "It's all there," she said, her voice barely a whisper. "The proof, the confession." She watched as Detective Ramirez flipped through the pages, her expression unreadable. The room felt small and suffocating, the walls closing in on them as they waited for her response.

The detective looked up, her eyes hard. "This is serious," she said. "If what you're saying is true, then your lives have been in danger from the start. We'll need to move quickly."

Julia nodded, the reality of the situation settling in her chest like a lead weight. "We know," she said, her voice barely above a whisper. "We'll do whatever it takes to make sure he can't hurt anyone else."

Chapter 16:

The detective stood, her gaze meeting Julia's. "I'll need you all to come down to the station and give formal statements," she said. "We'll need to verify everything you've told me."

Julia nodded, her mind racing with a whirlwind of emotions. The walls of the car seemed to close in on her as they drove back to the station, each of her friends lost in their own thoughts. When they arrived, they were led to separate rooms, the coldness of the building a stark contrast to the warmth of the night outside.

The moment she saw her father in handcuffs, Julia felt a part of her die. The man she had looked up to, the man who had taught her right from wrong, was now the very embodiment of what she had been fighting against. She watched as he was led away, his head bowed in defeat. The look in his eyes was one she had never seen before—fear, regret, and a desperate plea for understanding.

"Julia," he whispered as the officers pulled him away. "Please, tell your mother..." His words were lost in the chaos, but she knew what he meant. The secrets had been buried for too long, and now the truth had unearthed them like a tornado ripping through their lives.

Julia felt her knees give out as she watched her father being led away. The man who had held her hand on her first day of school, who had been there for every milestone in her life, was now a murderer. The room was spinning, the fluorescent lights above flickering like a sadistic strobe, highlighting the grim reality of the situation.

"I'm sorry," he whispered, his voice barely audible over the shuffling of feet and the murmur of the officers. "Please, tell your mother..." His words were a plea, a desperate attempt to hold onto the last shred of their relationship.

Julia felt a tear slip down her cheek as she watched the man who had been her rock crumble before her eyes. The man who had taught her to ride a bike, who had cheered her on at every soccer game, who had held her when she cried over her first heartbreak. The man who had been her hero. Now, in the harsh light of the police station, she saw him for what he truly was: a coward who had allowed fear to dictate his actions, leaving a trail of destruction in his wake.

Later that night, standing at Taylor's grave, the chilly wind whispering through the leaves, she realized that no matter what they had uncovered, the damage was done. The lies had fractured their friendship, leaving jagged edges that no apology could ever smooth over. The whispers of their past had grown into a roar that had shaken their very foundation, leaving them all forever changed.

The moon cast a pale light over the cemetery, casting long shadows that danced with the sway of the trees. Julia's eyes filled with tears as she stared at the simple headstone that marked the end of a life filled with so much potential. Taylor had been the one to keep them all together, the glue that bound their fractured hearts. Now, she was gone, a victim of their own game.

.

Don't miss out!

Visit the website below and you can sign up to receive emails whenever Art Vulcan publishes a new book. There's no charge and no obligation.

https://books2read.com/r/B-A-MJTMC-FPIDF

BOOKS 2 READ

Connecting independent readers to independent writers.

Milton Keynes UK
Ingram Content Group UK Ltd.
UKHW042236011124
450424UK00001BA/17